DANCING
ON THE TABLE

DANCING
ON THE TABLE

Liza Ketchum Murrow

drawings by
RONALD HIMLER

Holiday House / New York

Library of Congress Cataloging-in-Publication Data

Murrow, Liza Ketchum.
Dancing on the table / written by Liza Ketchum Murrow :
illustrated by Ronald Himler.—1st ed.
p. cm.
Summary: As Jenny doesn't want her grandmother to get married,
she makes two wishes on her lucky rabbit charm to ruin Nana's plans.
ISBN 0-8234-0808-6
[1. Grandmothers—Fiction. 2. Wishes—Fiction.] I. Himler,
Ronald. ill. II. Title.
PZ7.M96713Dan 1990
[Fic]—dc20   89-46066   CIP   AC

For the Harwells, who sang the songs,
and in memory of Weezie, who danced on the table

DANCING
ON THE TABLE

1

Crazy Legs

It was Saturday morning. Jenny Lawrence was building a fort under the big spruce tree. She dragged old boards from the woodpile near the shed and propped them up against the tree trunk. Down in the harbor, the boats had disappeared in the fog, but Jenny heard the deep chugging of her father's lobster boat close to shore. Suddenly a familiar horn tooted from the bottom of the hill and a car crossed the bridge onto Bright's Island. Jenny scrambled into her shelter to hide as an old green Dodge wheeled into the Lawrences' driveway.

When her grandmother's high heels clicked past on the walk, Jenny sang out, "Hey, Na-na."

Her grandmother's feet stopped. "Jenny?" Nana called. "Where are you?"

"In my fort." Jenny burst out of her hiding place, laughing. "Boo!"

Nana laughed her deep laugh. "Why, Jenny, you fooled me." Her eyes were bright.

"Is this a mischief day?" Jenny asked.

"It might be." Nana flicked pine needles from the thick wool of Jenny's sweater. "We haven't had one of our special Saturdays in a long time, have we?" She took Jenny's hand. "Better come inside first. I have a surprise for you."

Jenny ran ahead of her grandmother into the kitchen. Her little brother Morgan sat in his high chair. When he saw Nana, he slapped his palms on the metal tray and shouted, "Da!" Nana sat down at the table and tickled his round chin.

4

Jenny wedged herself between Morgan and her grandmother, squeezing into Nana's lap. "What's the surprise?" she begged. "Did you bring me something?"

"Are you going to tell her?" Jenny's mother asked, putting some cheese cubes on Morgan's tray.

"Tell me what?" Jenny cried, tugging at Nana's hands.

Nana's eyes danced. "Guess what I'm doing next month?"

Jenny laughed. How could she ever guess Nana's secrets? "I don't know," she said.

"I'm getting married," Nana announced.

Jenny stared. "*Grandmothers* don't get married."

Nana threw back her head and laughed. "This one does." She reached for Jenny's hand, but Jenny slipped off her grandmother's lap.

"Who are you getting married to?" Jenny whispered, but she knew the answer even before Nana said, "Why, Charlie, of course."

Jenny flopped on the floor and grabbed Max, the cat, by his fluffy tail, dragging him toward her. All summer long, Charlie Streeter had sat on her grandmother's front porch, smoking a pipe and laughing his big laugh while the lobstermen pulled their traps in the cove. When Mr. Streeter was there, Nana wore bright red lipstick and brushed her streaked hair high off her forehead.

Even though Mr. Streeter told Jenny to call him Uncle Charlie, she secretly thought of him as the Gray Man. Everything about him was gray: his hair and his rumpled suits, his eyes behind steel-rimmed glasses, even his little Honda sedan. And Jenny didn't like the way he showed off his old magic tricks—like always knowing which card she'd picked from a deck, even when she'd shuffled the cards right in front of him.

"Will *he* be my new grandfather?" Jenny demanded, glancing at Nana. Her grandmother had kicked off her shoes and

6

crossed one leg over the other; she swung her stockinged foot above Jenny's head.

"He certainly will," Nana said, "and he's so pleased—he doesn't have grandchildren of his own."

Jenny's mother put a plate of cookies on the table. "Won't that be nice, Jenny?" she asked.

Jenny didn't answer. She jumped up, grabbed a cookie, and sat back down on the rug, hauling Max into her lap.

Nana tugged Jenny's braid. "Don't be cross," she said. "Besides, there's another surprise."

"What?" Jenny asked without looking up. She crumbled her cookie and held the crumbs under Max's nose. The cat's rough tongue scraped across her fingers.

"Charlie and I want you to be the flower girl in our wedding," Nana said.

Jenny ate her broken cookie. "What does a flower girl do?" she asked with her mouth full.

"You'll walk down the aisle ahead of

me," Nana said, "carrying a bouquet of chrysanthemums. You'll wear a beautiful dress. Charlie and I will be so proud."

"I hate dresses," Jenny muttered, and she crawled under the table, curling up between the chair legs. "Why didn't you tell me before?" she demanded.

"We thought it would be too hard for you to wait," Nana said.

Jenny didn't say anything. Even though her father said eight was too old for thumb-sucking, she stuck her thumb in her mouth.

"Well, Mama," she heard her mother say, "I hope you behave yourself better at this wedding than at your last."

Jenny wiggled out from under the chair and twisted her head to look up at Nana. "What did you do?" she asked, forgetting to be cross.

Nana smiled. "Your mother always talks about my first wedding as though she'd been there!" Her grandmother took a bite from a chocolate chip cookie. "The party was such fun, I danced on the table. My parents were furious." Nana's eyes opened wide. "Imagine—dancing the Charleston right in the middle of Great-grandmother's best crystal goblets!"

"What's the Charleston?" Jenny asked.

"A dance," Nana answered, jumping up. She twitched her old wool skirt until her knees flashed. Her feet twisted and turned as her legs flew out to the side.

"Crazy Legs," Jenny's mother said when Nana stopped. "That's what they called your grandmother, Jenny. Crazy Legs Calvino."

"Calvino? Who's that?" Jenny asked.

"That was my name before I got married the first time," Nana said. Her cheeks were bright pink.

"It sounds like pizza sauce," Jenny said.

"Jenny . . ." her mother warned, but Nana laughed.

"You're right," she said. "I'm part Italian." Then Nana's face got sad and far away. She looked at Jenny's mother. "Bea,

10

you know I love Charlie," Nana said, "but it's not the same as Phillip."

Jenny knew Nana meant her grandpa Phil, who died before she was born. For a minute, she thought Nana and her mother might cry.

"Will there be dancing at this wedding?" Jenny asked quickly.

"I should hope so," Nana said. "Especially with the cousins here."

"The cousins are coming?" Jenny scrambled to her feet.

"Of course," Nana said. "They wouldn't miss my wedding."

Jenny climbed up onto the table, pushing the dishes aside. She waved her arms and stamped her feet.

"Jenny!" her mother scolded. "What are you doing?"

"Crazy Legs, Crazy Legs, dance all night!" Jenny sang. Her shoes drummed the table. The plate of cookies bounced and Morgan's milk tipped over. Nana jumped up and reached for a napkin.

11

"Look, Morgan, I'm dancing!" Jenny cried. She clicked her heels and almost lost her balance. Morgan squealed and pounded his tray.

"Jenny, get down this minute," her mother said in a sharp voice.

"I'm just practicing for the wedding." But Jenny slid onto the floor, scooped up Max, and set him in the pool of milk. "Lick it up, kitty," she said. Max's long tail twitched. He shook his paws and lapped the milk.

Jenny's mother gave Jenny a sponge to wipe the table. "Jenny, what are we going to do with you?"

"Steal her away to make some mischief," Nana said. "Come on, Miss Jenny, we've got something important to do."

Nana leaned toward Morgan, stuck her finger into her cheek, and pulled it out with a loud pop. "See you later, munchkin," she said. She hurried out the door and tripped down the walk, with Jenny trotting beside her to keep up.

2

The Lucky Charm

Jenny settled herself in the front seat of Nana's rattly car and sat on her hands to keep them still. Where would they go today? Nana used to take her someplace every Saturday. Sometimes they drove the eight miles to Nana's house at the far end of the island and went on night walks, sneaking across the neighbors' lawns. Once they collected mussels at low tide and made a driftwood campfire in Nana's rocky cove. Last spring they went to Portland to see one of Maine's baseball teams play in a night game. Nana let Jenny have hot dogs and candy for dinner. Then Mr. Streeter started coming around, and Nana didn't have time for mischief days.

Nana drove over the causeway joining Bright's Island to the mainland and turned away from the ocean.

"Where are we going?" Jenny asked.

Nana laughed and tossed her head. The white streak in her hair looked like the stripe on a skunk's back. "You'll see. Can you find some good music?"

Jenny switched on the radio and tuned in Nana's country music station. A woman sang a song about a honky-tonk angel. Nana hummed along.

They drove along the back road and then out to the main highway. "Are we going to Stone Harbor?" Jenny asked.

"Maybe." Nana turned the radio up loud. "Listen—the cousins do this one," she said. It was a song about a hobo who was going down the road carrying one thin dime. Jenny joined in on the chorus.

14

The Lucky Charm

Pretty soon, they were on Stone Harbor's main street. Nana turned at the traffic light and parked behind an old brick building. Jenny got out and followed her grandmother up some dark stairs. The door on the landing had a dusty window with rippled glass. When Nana knocked, a small woman with short, black hair let them in. A row of pins and needles bristled on the collar of her blouse. She greeted Nana, then smiled at Jenny and cried, "So this is the little one!"

"Jenny, this is Mrs. Sambota," Nana said. "She's making your dress for the wedding."

Mrs. Sambota reached for Jenny's hand, but Jenny pulled away and looked around the tiny room. Dresses and skirts hung from curtain rods and scraps of fabric littered the floor.

"Your dress is over there," the woman said, pointing toward the window. Two cardboard bodies shaped like women without arms, legs, or heads stood in the cor-

15

ner. Next to them was a smaller model, no bigger than Jenny, wearing a party dress with long sleeves. The dress was chocolate brown, covered with tiny yellow flowers. "So pretty, with your chestnut hair," Mrs. Sambota said, lifting the dress off the model. "But I didn't know your size. Let's try it on."

"Now?" Jenny asked. She glanced at Nana.

"Of course," Nana said. "Take off your clothes. You can slip it on right here."

Before she knew what was happening, Jenny was standing in her underwear in the middle of the room and Mrs. Sambota was lowering the dress over her head. "Ow!" Jenny cried, as pins pricked her back and arms.

"Sorry," Mrs. Sambota said, "I didn't want to sew it up until I checked the fit. Now." She turned Jenny around so she could see herself in a long mirror.

Jenny scowled. The sleeves dangled way below her arms and the skirt drooped around her legs. "It's ugly," she said, turning away from the mirror.

"Why, Jenny," Nana scolded, "that's rude. Apologize to Mrs. Sambota."

Jenny clenched her mouth tight.

To her surprise, Mrs. Sambota said, "She's right. It's much too big. Hold still now, and we'll fix it." She took pins from her mouth, pinching the material here and there, turning Jenny back and forth until finally she said briskly, "All done. Come back in a few days for another fitting."

Jenny got dressed, ran down the stairs ahead of Nana, and stood by the car, waiting to get in. Her grandmother shook her head. "It's not time to go home yet," she said. "Come on, we're going to get rid of that frown."

They walked down the main street to O'Leary's ice-cream parlor. Nana opened the door but Jenny stood frozen on the sidewalk. A small gray Honda was parked in front. "That's Mr. Streeter's car," Jenny said, backing away from her grandmother.

17

"Why, so it is," Nana said. "Now I wonder what he could be doing here?"

"I don't like Mr. Streeter," Jenny announced in a loud voice.

Nana closed the door to the shop and planted her feet on the sidewalk in front of Jenny. Her dark eyes flashed and Jenny knew she meant business. "You don't have to like him. But I expect you to be polite, starting right now," Nana said.

Jenny didn't answer. She dragged her feet going inside. The Gray Man was waiting for them at a booth. Jenny dropped onto the bench without saying hello. Nana sat down next to Charlie Streeter.

"Well," Mr. Streeter said, "what did you think of our news?"

"It's okay." Jenny flipped the jukebox cards on the wall beside her. The Gray Man reached across the table, pulled at Jenny's ear, and said, "Look what I found." A quarter lay in his pudgy hand. "Don't you ever wash your ears?" he asked, giving her the quarter, but Jenny wouldn't smile. She punched the buttons for the jukebox without even looking at the names of the songs.

When the waitress came, Mr. Streeter ordered a coffee milk shake. "I shouldn't," he said, smiling at the waitress and patting his round belly, "but we're celebrating today. Lucinda, what will you have?"

Jenny glared at him. "Her name is Nana," she said.

"Jenny—" Nana warned, but the Gray Man laughed.

"I know she's 'Nana' to you, hon," he said, "but Lucinda's such a pretty name, don't you think?" He pinched Nana's cheek softly until she gave him a crooked smile.

Jenny couldn't see why her grandmother should be cross one minute and goofy the next. Was this what happened when you got married?"

"What would you like, Jen?" Nana asked, smiling as if everything was all right again. "Since we're making mischief,

19

maybe we'd better share a banana split."

"It's not a mischief day when Mr. Streeter's here," Jenny announced.

Charlie Streeter's eyes blinked fast, like lights switching on and off, and Nana exclaimed, "Jenny—that's just what we were talking about outside."

Jenny turned to the waitress as if she hadn't heard. "I want my own banana split. With coffee, vanilla, and fudge swirl ice cream."

"Don't be wasteful," Nana scolded.

Mr. Streeter patted Nana's hand. "It's my treat," he said. "Let her have what she wants."

While they waited for their food, Jenny watched her grandmother. Nana was silly around the Gray Man. She kept flicking her hair off her collar and swinging her leg under the table. She laughed too loud and leaned her head on Mr. Streeter's shoulder. When Nana's ice cream came she fed the Gray Man little tastes with her spoon.

Jenny felt lonesome on her side of the

booth. She ate her coffee ice cream, then part of the vanilla. She made tracks in the chocolate sauce with her spoon and piled the whipped cream up at one end of the banana.

"You'll have to come visit us," Mr. Streeter was saying to Jenny. She stared at him, then at her grandmother.

"He means in New York," Nana said. "Charlie lives in New York City, remember?"

"You're moving to New York?" Jenny asked. She pushed her dish away.

"Not forever," Nana said. "When Charlie retires, we'll come back to Maine, and we'll still be here summers and weekends. Don't worry, nutkin, I'll never sell my house. Besides, you can visit us in New York. We'll take you to the circus—"

"I *hate* the circus!" Jenny exploded. "It's boring."

Nana threw up her hands. "Jenny, you're impossible today!"

Jenny wasn't listening. She flopped

21

down sideways and let her braid dangle over the bench. Something white caught her eye. She reached down and scooped it off the floor. It was a rabbit's foot on a chain. Jenny smoothed the soft fur with her thumb, then held it against her cheek.

"Someone must have left that here," Nana said. "Maybe you should give it to the waitress."

"Wait a minute," Charlie Streeter said. Jenny and Nana both stared at him, surprised.

"A rabbit's foot is a lucky charm," he said. "If Jenny found it, she was meant to have it." He smiled at Jenny. "You can clip it to your belt and use it whenever you need good luck. Something you have to remember, though—most wishes come in threes. I'll bet that's true for this charm."

"How do *you* know?" Jenny asked rudely.

Charlie Streeter shrugged. "I know a little bit about magic," he said.

Three wishes. Jenny looked at her

23

grandmother, then at Mr. Streeter. His round eyes twinkled behind his glasses.

She hooked the little chain through her belt and rubbed the white fur. It was silky and warm.

"Well?" Nana said. "What will you wish?"

"If I tell you, the wish won't work," Jenny said.

"She's right," the Gray Man said, nodding. "Secrecy is very important."

Jenny tossed her braid behind her shoulder and closed her eyes. She'd save her wishes for the wedding day. And then she'd show the Gray Man how magic *really* worked.

3

The Cousins

The morning of the wedding, Jenny sat at her grandmother's kitchen table. Nana's house was on a point at the south end of Bright's Island, and usually Jenny perched near the window to watch the lobster boats bobbing beyond the rocks. Today, she kept her eyes on her grandmother. Nana was rushing around in her bathrobe. Her teacup rattled in her hand and her blue slippers scuffed on the bare floor.

"Where's my coffee?" Nana's voice came out high and squeaky, like an old fiddle.

"You're carrying it," Jenny said.

Nana looked down. "Why, so I am." She took a quick sip, set the cup down, and looked out the window. "Jenny—the cousins are here! Would you look at that black cloud—and where on earth did I put my rings?"

Nana ran out onto the porch, holding her robe together with one hand. "Sarah! Teddy!" she called. "What are you thinking, bringing a storm?"

Jenny pushed past her grandmother and ran down the walk as her southern cousins tumbled out of a big station wagon. Cody, who was sixteen, scooped Jenny up and twirled her around.

"Hi, sugar," said Cody's mom, Great-Aunt Sarah, when Jenny was set on her feet again. "Hello, honey," said Great-Aunt Grace. Sarah and Grace were Nana's younger sisters. They bent to kiss Jenny's head, then hurried to hug Nana. Jenny's great-uncle Teddy unfolded himself from the front seat. His blue eyes twinkled

26

behind his glasses. "Jenny, look how you've grown!" he said, tweaking her long braid.

"Did you bring your guitars?" Jenny asked.

"Did we ever," said Cody. He opened the back of the station wagon. Guitars, suitcases, and clothes were all jumbled together. He pulled out a tiny case and snapped it open. "A ukelele," he said, "just the right size for you. Try it."

Jenny loved the way the cousins talked. Their voices made songs when they said "y'all," and "y'hear?" She took the small wooden instrument and brushed her fingers across the strings. The ukelele squeaked and twanged. "Mind your own bizniss," Jenny sang, strumming hard.

" 'Bizniss?' " Cody laughed. "Who taught you that southern talk?"

"Nana, let's sing!" Jenny cried. Nana and her sisters were all talking at once. They sounded like squirrels chattering.

"Not now, hon. After the wedding," said

Nana. A gust of wind tugged at Nana's dressing gown and grabbed Aunt Sarah's wide-brimmed hat. It sailed into the bushes like a big red bird; Aunt Sarah's soft hair whipped across her face.

Jenny scrambled into the prickers and pulled out the hat. "Thanks, sugar," Aunt Sarah said. She looked into Jenny's face, then at Nana. "Why, Cinda, this child looks more like you all the time. She's got your big dark eyes, full of mischief." She smiled at Jenny. "Tell me, what do y'all think about your grandma running away with a trickster like Charlie Streeter?"

Before Jenny could say she didn't like it a bit, another gust of wind made the aunts scream and hold their skirts.

Uncle Teddy whistled. "Storm's coming. Hoo-ee!" he cried. "Better get this wedding moving, Lucinda. Heard on the radio that Hurricane Wanda's moving up the coast."

"*Wanda!*" Nana cried. Her dark eyes

snapped, but she laughed. "I never heard of such nonsense. Don't you talk like that, Teddy. You know I don't allow hurricanes on my wedding day."

A hurricane? Jenny looked at the sky. The clouds were a strange dark green color, like the slippery seaweed that covered the rocks in the cove.

When everyone started up the walk, Jenny ran to the back of the house and down the hill to the water. Waves were pounding the little beach where she and Nana always swam. The wind was making frothy whitecaps all over the bay and tugging at the lobster boats, resting at their moorings.

Jenny squinched her eyes shut and remembered pictures she'd seen in a magazine of a hurricane in Florida. Palm trees were bent to the ground and waves smashed over the roof of a house. No one could go anywhere in a hurricane, could they? Jenny heard Cody calling her, his voice all hollow in the wind. She felt for the rabbit's foot, dangling from her belt. "This is my first wish," she whispered, clutching the fur. "Bring Wanda to Bright's Island so Nana will stay here with me forever."

4

Something Borrowed, Something Blue

It was time to get dressed. Jenny was in Nana's bedroom with her mother, Aunt Sarah, and Aunt Grace. Morgan sat on the floor, holding one of Nana's shoes in his mouth.

"Don't!" Jenny hissed. She grabbed the shoe, and Morgan howled.

"Hush the baby, can't you?" Nana said. She sat at her dressing table in a black slip, powdering her nose.

Jenny gave the shoe to Morgan. He scuttled under Nana's bed, dragging it by a shiny black strap.

"Jenny, let's put your dress on," her mother said.

Jenny took off her jeans and sweater, then stood still while her mother dropped the soft material over her head and zipped her up.

"Ouch." Jenny wiggled until she was all inside the dress. Her mother looped the sash around Jenny's waist and tied it in a bow. "You look wonderful," her mother said.

"I hate getting dressed up," Jenny complained, but when she turned to face Nana's tall mirror, someone different looked out at her: a thin girl with big dark eyes and flushed cheeks. The dress made her look older and taller. Jenny smoothed the soft skirt. The yellow flowers winked like lights against their dark background. When Jenny twirled, the skirt billowed out below her knees. She frowned.

If Wanda came, could she still wear the dress?

"Jenny, what's that long face for?" Aunt Grace said. "Come here and let me brush your hair."

While Aunt Grace undid her braid and combed through the tangles, Jenny looked out the window. The tall spruce trees were swaying in the wind.

"Look, Mom—the wind's making the trees dance," Jenny cried. But her mother was listening to Nana.

"The rain will spoil my dress," Nana wailed. "My hair will be ruined—I'll look dreadful."

"You'll be beautiful, Mama," Jenny's mother said. "Don't worry." She hugged Nana.

Jenny bit her lip. Was her wish really working? What would Nana say if she knew Jenny was making it storm?

Great-Aunt Sarah sat on Nana's bed, swinging her long, thin legs. "I'm sure you'll be the belle of the ball, Lucinda."

34

Aunt Sarah's chuckle was soft and warm.

"What's the belle of a ball?" Jenny asked.

Her great-aunts laughed, and her mother said, "That means she'll be the most popular girl at the party."

"Not if she doesn't get ready." Aunt Grace stretched to take Nana's dress down from the canopy of her big four-poster bed. "Stand up, Lucinda," she said, "you shouldn't keep Charlie waiting."

When the dress was settled on Nana's shoulders, everyone was quiet. Jenny stared. Her grandmother looked beautiful. Nana's bright, soft eyes matched her auburn dress. Jenny ran to her grandmother and put her arms around Nana's waist. "Don't go away," she whispered.

Nana smoothed her hair. "I know it's hard, hon. But it's an adventure for me. A chance to kick up my heels and have fun." She shuffled her stockinged feet, jumped in the air, and threw her legs to the side, trying to kick her heels together.

"Whoops—I missed!" she said, landing with a thud.

"Lucinda," Aunt Grace said, "behave yourself."

"Not on your life," Nana laughed. She cupped Jenny's chin in her hand. "Give us a smile. It's not forever."

But Jenny shivered. She'd heard what they'd said yesterday at the rehearsal: "Till death us do part."

"You ladies almost ready?" Someone knocked on the bedroom door. Jenny ran to open it. Her father stood in the hall. He was wearing a suit, but his tie was undone and his straight blond hair was rumpled and wild. Behind him was a big man with a thick, bristling beard and shining eyes.

"What's the matter?" the man cried, in a deep voice. "Don't you recognize your uncle Teto?"

Jenny squealed and ran into his arms. Teto hoisted her up onto his shoulder, tickling her cheek with his new beard. Then he set her down and threw his arms

37

around Jenny's mother. "Hey, sis," he said, "are you shrinking, or am I still growing?"

Jenny's mother laughed. She looked tiny in her brother's arms.

"Teto!" Nana cried. "Scrape that rat's nest off your face this minute!" But she was laughing and hugging him.

Teto kissed Nana. "Calm down, Mama," he said. "If I shave, the girls will see my ugly chin."

Jenny giggled. Teto was a bachelor. Sometimes he brought his girlfriends to Maine to meet Nana. Even the friendly ones were shy around her grandmother.

Jenny's father cleared his throat. "Come on, ladies, it's almost time."

Teto rummaged in his pocket, pulled out a bright elastic ribbon, and tossed it to Nana. "Here you go, Mama," he said. "Something blue. Throw it to me later so I can be the next one married." He winked at Jenny and closed the door.

"What is it?" Jenny asked.

"A garter," said Aunt Grace, "to wear around her leg. Go ahead, Lucinda, put it on."

Nana slipped the blue elastic over her small foot and pulled it up above her knee. Then her sisters fussed over her dress. They combed Nana's hair and clasped her pearls. When no one was looking, Jenny took the rabbit's foot off her belt and hooked it through her sash. Then she sat down on the floor. Her grandmother's shoe sat alone on the rug, waiting for Nana. Jenny pushed it toward Morgan, who was still playing under Nana's bed. He cooed, rolled onto his back, and banged the shoes together.

"Where are my shoes?" Nana cried. Aunt Sarah started rummaging through Nana's clothes, heaped over the chairs and the bed. Aunt Grace looked in the closet. Jenny's mother opened Nana's suitcase and started taking things out. "Which ones are they?" Jenny's mother asked.

"My new pair," Nana said. She sounded cross. "You know—the black ones. I don't have anything else. I'll have to go bare-foot."

"Take it easy, Mama," Jenny's mother said, but she looked upset.

Jenny sighed. She reached under Nana's bed and grabbed the shoes from her brother. Morgan screamed and crawled out after her.

"Here they are," Jenny said. "Morgan took them." Jenny's mother gave her a funny look, but she didn't say anything. Nana grabbed the shoes and stuffed her feet inside. When she picked up her brush, her hand froze above her head.

"Something borrowed, something blue," she said. "Quick, someone, what can I do?"

"What does that mean?" Jenny asked.

Aunt Sarah smoothed Jenny's hair. "It's just a saying. If you wear something bor-rowed and something blue on your wed-

40

ding day, it brings you good luck. Here, Lucinda," she said, taking off the gold butterfly pinned to her collar, "wear this. But don't lose it."

"*That* thing?" Nana said. "You know it's too clunky for me." But she let Aunt Sarah pin the butterfly on her dress.

Jenny's mother laughed. "No fighting today, ladies," she said. "Go on, leave your sister alone for a minute."

Aunt Sarah smiled at Jenny. "Want to come with me, sugar?" Jenny shook her head and the aunts left the room.

Jenny's mother scooped up Morgan, who was whining and fussing. "Let's go, crosspatch," she said. "Time to get your best suit on. Jenny, let Nana have a minute alone."

"Alone!" Nana cried. "Don't leave me now! Jenny, you stay right here. I need someone to help me finish packing."

Jenny took Nana's dresses from their hangers and handed them to her grandmother. Nana's brown leather bag bulged and creaked. Nana sighed. "It will never close. And Charlie will have a fit if I bring another suitcase on our honeymoon."

"Is a honeymoon like a mischief day?" Jenny asked.

Nana shook her head. "Only you and I have mischief days," she said, pulling Jenny close.

"Can I come on your honeymoon?" Jenny asked, her voice muffled against Nana's dress.

"I'm afraid not," Nana said.

"Why?" Jenny pulled away and climbed onto Nana's tall bed.

"A honeymoon's just for the two people who get married." Nana fiddled with her suitcase. "This bag will never shut. Could you get out my duffel?"

Jenny slithered under the bed and came out with a long bag shaped like a sausage. When Nana went into her closet for more clothes, Jenny pulled down the zipper and crawled inside the duffel. She just fit, with her knees scrunched up.

"Surprise!" she said, popping out at her grandmother.

Nana jumped, then cocked her head to one side. "You don't want me to get married, do you?" she said.

"Yes I do," Jenny said, but she looked away. Lying made her feel hot inside, as if she'd swallowed scalding cocoa.

Uncle Teto called from downstairs, "Mama! Jenny! It's time."

Jenny looked at her grandmother. Nana's soft face was pinched. "Maybe you're right," Nana whispered. "Maybe I'm nuts."

Jenny held her breath. Would Nana change her mind? But her grandmother took a deep breath and stood up straight. "What am I thinking about?" she said softly to herself. "Come on, Lucinda, pull yourself together." She gave Jenny a small, almost frightened smile and said, "Goodness, will you listen to that wind?"

43

5

The Wedding

Big drops of rain splattered on the slate walk; the trees danced and swayed. When Jenny ran to the car, her skirt ballooned into the air and her cousin Peter whistled.

"I see London, I see France, I see Jenny's under—"

"Hush!" said Aunt Sarah. "Don't embarrass her."

Cody was wearing a suit and tie. His hair was slicked down. He opened the car door for Jenny as if she were a lady. "You're sure looking pretty," he said. Jenny felt too shy to answer, even though Cody was her favorite cousin.

"Where's Nana?" she whispered, as she squeezed into the car.

"She's coming, honey," said Uncle Teddy. "We're always waiting on your grandma, but she's never disappointed us yet."

"She'll be comin' round the mountain when she comes," Peter sang low under his breath.

As if she heard him, Nana came tripping down the walk, holding her hat tight on her head. She got in the car with Jenny's mother and father. Everyone in Uncle Teddy's station wagon sang all the way to the church.

"Run between the raindrops!" Cody cried, as they raced up the slick stone steps.

Uncle Teddy hushed them at the door. "Y'all calm down now," he said.

When he opened the heavy doors, Jenny felt solemn. An organ was playing softly,

45

and the first few rows were filled with people. Aunt Sarah gave Jenny her bouquet of flowers and smoothed her hair. Cody took her coat and put it on a hanger. "Isn't she precious?" Aunt Grace whispered, adjusting Jenny's sash.

Jenny wished she were home, playing with Max. She wished she were under Nana's canopy bed, opening her grandmother's round hatboxes and trying on the old-fashioned hats. Why wasn't Wanda here yet? Maybe Charlie Streeter was only joking about the magic in the rabbit's foot.

The organ started to play loud, cheerful music. All the relatives went to sit behind Jenny's father, who was holding Morgan in the first pew.

Far away, standing beside tall vases filled with orange and yellow flowers, was the Gray Man. He was smiling, and his hands were folded over his stomach. His best friend stood beside him. Jenny had met him at the rehearsal. The two men wore matching gray suits with little white flowers in the lapels. They were both tall and round: Tweedledum and Tweedledee, Jenny thought with a grin. Her mother gave her a little push. "Now," she whispered.

Jenny started down the aisle. She followed the dark red rug, holding her flowers tight. She walked slowly, the way the minister had told her. It took a long time to reach the front of the church. Her new shoes squeaked as she stepped onto the wood floor, and when she passed Morgan, he squealed and waved his arms at her. Everyone laughed.

Jenny stood by the altar and watched her mother come down the aisle. She was Nana's matron of honor. Her dress was the color of the sand on Nana's beach and her eyes were shiny; Jenny couldn't tell if she was happy or sad. Then the organ music filled the church and Nana came through the door, holding Uncle Teto's arm. She looked worried, even scared. Jenny couldn't help smiling at her grandmother,

and Nana's eyes twinkled for an instant before she turned to take the Gray Man's hand.

The wind rattled the tall church windows. Jenny clutched her flowers and waited for her wish to come true. Instead, the minister started talking. He recited a prayer and then said, in a complicated way, that if anyone knew a reason why Nana and the Gray Man shouldn't get married, "let him now speak . . ."

The minister's deep, solemn voice seemed to vibrate from the rafters. He waited for a long second and the whole church held its breath. Jenny looked around. Would someone stop the wedding? Jenny opened her mouth. She could think of *lots* of reasons why the wedding shouldn't happen. She wanted to shout, but her tongue was dry and her lips wouldn't move. The minister smiled, Uncle Teto stepped aside, and before Jenny knew it, her grandmother was married to the Gray Man.

6

"Just Married"

After the wedding, Jenny ran back and forth from the kitchen to the laundry room, carrying wet coats and hats. The kitchen door kept banging and flapping in the wind as Nana's friends rushed in. Rain dripped from their coats, and their boots left puddles on the tiled floor. The house filled with loud talk.

Nana's friends brought hot vegetable casseroles, loaves of bread, and bowls of fruit. Jenny grabbed a handful of crackers from the long table in the dining room and stuffed one into her mouth. Starting around the corner with a bundle of coats under her arm, she bumped into Charlie Streeter.

"Oops," said Jenny. "Sorry." She tried to get past him, but he held her arm gently.

"Wait, Jenny, I need your help with something. Can you keep a secret?"

"Sometimes," Jenny said carefully.

The Gray Man chuckled. "That's an honest answer."

Jenny finished her cracker and looked down at the Gray Man's plump hand, resting on her sleeve. His new wedding ring was shiny below his knuckle.

Charlie Streeter glanced around the living room. The guests were clustered near the punch bowl, their voices buzzing. "Can you come here for a minute?" he asked. Jenny followed him into the laundry room. They stacked the coats on the washing machine and then the Gray Man patted his suit pocket. "I've got a surprise for your grandmother. I was going to put it in her suitcase, but her sisters wouldn't let me up there." He pointed toward the back stairs.

Jenny frowned. "How did you know where her room was?" she asked suspiciously.

Charlie Streeter cleared his throat, then took off his glasses and wiped them on the sleeve of his suit. "I've been upstairs a few times, hon."

Jenny didn't like him calling her "hon," and she didn't care about his surprise. But the Gray Man was pulling a fat manila envelope out of his pocket. "Anyway, I decided to stick these in the car, but your uncle Teto wouldn't let me. I'm afraid he's cooked up some devilish plan for my Honda."

Jenny shifted awkwardly from one foot to the other. She wanted to get back to the cousins, but Mr. Streeter kept right on talking. "You did a beautiful job in the wedding," he was saying, settling his glasses back on his nose. "I'm proud to have you for a new granddaughter. Do you think you can call me 'Uncle Charlie' now?"

"Okay," Jenny mumbled, but inside her head a voice chanted, *Gray Man, Gray Man*. She cocked her head; someone was tuning a guitar in the next room. Would she miss the singing?

"Don't worry." Charlie Streeter acted as if he knew what she was thinking. "This won't take long." He opened the long envelope. "We're flying to New York tonight. Your grandmother thinks we're staying there for our honeymoon, but in fact, I'm taking her to San Francisco tomorrow." His small eyes grew bright behind his glasses. "She's always wanted to go out West. And I thought, why not now?" He smiled. "I was hoping you could put these brochures in the car. Maybe in the glove compartment—you know how she's always rummaging around in there, looking for my peppermints?"

Jenny didn't like the way he knew about Nana's little habits. And if he was so good at magic tricks, why couldn't he get the brochures in the car himself? But she remembered Nana's warning about being rude, so she took the stack of folders and asked, "Is it a long way to San Francisco?"

He nodded. "About as far from Maine as you can get, unless you go to Alaska." He pecked her cheek. "Thanks for your help. The car's in the shed." He started for the door.

"Mr. Streeter—"

"Uncle Charlie."

Jenny couldn't say that name. It stuck in her throat like raw spinach. "Umm—" she stuttered, "how long will you be gone?"

"On our trip? Just two weeks. I wish it could be longer."

Jenny was afraid to ask if they'd go straight to New York after that. When he left the room, she looked at the folders. One showed a picture of a big, red-gold bridge. In another brochure, people were hanging from the side of a trolley car as it climbed a steep hill.

A gust of wind shook Nana's house, and the windows rattled. Rain drummed on the porch roof, and the lights flickered off and on. Aunt Sarah's deep voice cried out in the kitchen.

"Come on, Wanda," Jenny whispered. She took her raincoat from her special hook in Nana's laundry room and went outside. The rain was streaming down. She ran across the driveway to the old shed. When she reached the Gray Man's car, her braid was soaked, and her new shoes were spattered with mud.

"Oh!" Jenny gasped, surprised. Some-one was bent over in the shadows at the back of the car. She almost ran away, until she realized it was Uncle Teto.

"Why, Jenny," he said, standing up. His dark hair was plastered to his round fore-head. He was almost shouting; the rain was pounding on the shed roof. "Just the person I need. Want to help me soup up the getaway car?"

Jenny grinned. "What are you doing?"

"A little bit of decorating. Come and look."

Jenny went to the back of the car. Teto handed her a flashlight so she could see the soda cans and plastic milk cartons dangling from the bumper. There was even an old lobster pot; Jenny recognized one of her father's traps.

Jenny giggled. "Will they be able to go anywhere?"

"Sure," Uncle Teto said, "but these cans will make a fine racket. Not that anyone will hear it, over this wind." He stared through the open door at the rain. It was blowing back and forth like the old curtains in Nana's living room. "I don't know about this storm," Teto said. "If it was me, I'd stay put, but I'm sure Mama wouldn't dream of waiting for the weather to clear. She believes planes will fly through anything." He frowned and scratched his

thick beard. "It's sure weird, helping your own mother get married."

Jenny shifted her weight from side to side. Had Uncle Teto forgotten she was there?

He slapped his face lightly. "Snap out of it," he commanded himself, then grinned at Jenny. His blue eyes twinkled. "I've got a job for you." He went behind the car and came back with a long piece of cardboard and some fat Magic Markers, including one with a bright silver top.

"You're making a sign—please, Uncle Teto, can I help?" Jenny begged.

"Absolutely." Uncle Teto propped the cardboard against the bumper and leaned over, drawing big, sloppy letters in red and green. "We're going to tease them a little—treat them like kids."

"Let me try," Jenny said, reaching for the pens.

Teto nodded. "Hold on— There. *Just Married*. Now, you take this outlining pen. Draw around the letters, and decorate it. Make some crazy designs."

"Just Married"

As Jenny took the markers she asked, "Uncle Teto—do you think wishes can come true?"

"Sometimes, if you wish hard enough, and if it's really important. Why? Do you have a special wish?"

"Uh-huh," Jenny said.

A car drove past and Uncle Teto peered out to watch it go by. "That's old Mrs. Slocum. She'll never make it to the house alone." He tipped his head at Jenny. "I'd better go help her."

"I'll finish this," Jenny said.

"Will you put the sign in the car when you're done?" Uncle Teto asked. "Lean it up against the back window, so people can read the words from the outside."

"I can do it," Jenny said, "don't worry."

"I never worry about you!" Uncle Teto exclaimed, giving her raincoat a little slap. Before Jenny could ask what he meant, he was out in the rain, jumping the deep puddles.

When he was out of sight Jenny took the

top off the black marker and crossed out the word "Just," then wrote the letters *N-O-T*. *"Not married,"* she whispered out loud. Her tongue worked back and forth across her lips as she outlined the letters in silver. She drew a fat green rabbit on one end of the sign and a cat like Max on the other. She opened the car door, wrestled the sign onto the back window ledge, climbed out, and studied it a minute. "Not married," she said again, raising her voice over the storm.

Jenny picked up the envelope full of brochures, took a deep breath, and ran out into the rain. She stumbled around the house and down the slippery path to the cove. Waves were pounding the rocks, and Nana's little beach was covered with water all the way to the edge of the lawn. The wind made Jenny's breath come out in hiccups. She scrambled onto a big rock, drew her arm back, and threw the manila envelope into the sea. The wind tore it open and the bright folders disappeared immediately, sucked into the boiling foam.

Jenny unzipped her coat and clutched the rabbit's foot at her waist. She stood with her legs braced against the wind. "Here's my second wish!" she yelled into the storm. "Make the hurricane stronger. Don't let Nana leave Bright's Island."

As if it heard her, the wind roared and whipped at Jenny's coat. She gasped, ducked her head, and ran for the house.

7

"Mind your own business"

Jenny put her coat away and hurried upstairs to Nana's bedroom. She left her wet dress on the floor, wiggled into her sweatshirt and blue jeans, and put the rabbit's foot back on her belt. She went downstairs feeling more like herself.

Outside the sitting room, Jenny heard Cody calling, but she couldn't see him at first. The cozy room was packed with Nana's friends and relatives. Forks chattered against plates; everyone was talking and laughing. Nana and Charlie Streeter stood in front of the fireplace. The Gray Man leaned against the mantel, with one arm draped over Nana's shoulder. A warm fire popped behind them. A camera flashed as Uncle Teddy took their picture.

Jenny sidled into the room. Charlie Streeter gave her the thumbs-up sign but Jenny pretended not to see him. She picked her way through tight knots of people, careful not to jostle any elbows. Cody sat on a small couch, strumming his guitar. "Time for songs, to drive away the storm," he said.

Peter came over and squeezed in beside them. His bushy hair stood up all over his head and his sweater was wet. "Whew—I ran outside to help an old lady out of her car. She almost blew away!" He took a bite of a ham sandwich. "Aunt Grace says Wanda's here for sure."

"Really?" Cody tightened a string until it hummed under his thumb. "Wonder why it came this way? They said it would go out to sea. I guess Wanda heard how

Aunt Lucinda always does things with a bang."

Jenny swallowed. Even though the rabbit's foot was hanging from her belt, she felt as if it were burning against her skin. "Maybe we'll have a tidal wave," she said, thinking about her second wish.

Peter sneered. "They don't have tidal waves in *Maine*, dummy."

"Y'all watch the way you talk to Jenny." Cody put his hand on Jenny's knee. Her cheeks burned. She wanted to cuddle up to him, but she didn't dare.

"I saw you running around down by the beach," Peter said. "What were you doing?"

"None of your business," Jenny snapped.

"Uh-oh—who's in a bad mood?" Peter teased.

"Hush," Cody said. He smiled at Jenny. "You put me in mind of a song." He played some chords on the guitar and settled the strap over his shoulder.

Jenny recognized the tune. *"Why don't you mind your own business?"* she sang,

glaring at Peter. The talking stopped; Aunt Grace and Uncle Teddy joined in on the next verse.

Nana clapped her hands. Her eyes were shining. "My favorite!" she cried, and everyone laughed.

The Gray Man pulled Nana onto his knees and swayed from side to side. "Let's hear you sing, Cinda," he said. He beamed when Nana's rich voice joined in:

"If I want to honky-tonk around 'til two or three,
Now brother, that's my headache, don't you worry 'bout me.
Why don't you mind your own business?
Mind your own business. . .
If you mind your business, then you won't be mindin' mine!"

Everyone laughed. Cody changed chords and they sang "The Fox," "She'll Be Comin' Round the Mountain," and

"Mind your own business"

"Working on the Railroad." Uncle Teddy sang his silly song about the pilot who was hanging from a telegraph pole. His scratchy voice made everyone laugh.

They sang the songs that Jenny's father called "the southern tunes": they were all about Jesus, and dying, and what would happen in the "sweet bye and bye." Jenny remembered most of the words, even though she didn't always know what they meant. She sang so hard, she almost forgot about the storm, and Nana leaving.

Then Jenny's mother and father and all the cousins started to whisper together. Uncle Teddy cleared his throat and pulled out a rumpled piece of paper.

"Someone here wrote a little tune about Charlie and Lucinda," he said. "If y'all are patient, we'll see if we can sing louder than Wanda."

As if the storm heard, the wind rattled around the side of the house, and rain beat on the windowpanes. Nana laughed. "Must be a powerful song!"

Jenny took Morgan from her mother and bounced him on her lap while Uncle Teddy tuned his banjo. All the guests crowded into the sitting room to hear the toast to Nana and Charlie. The song warned Uncle Charlie about Nana's habits: how she liked to sleep late; how she'd talk to her sisters for hours on the phone. And in the last verse, they sang:

"Charlie Streeter, are you able,
To manage a gal who dances on the table?"

Nana's friends clapped and cheered. Nana was tapping her heels and laughing.

"Don't give her any ideas!" Aunt Grace cried.

Suddenly there was a crash outside, louder than all the cymbals and drums smashing together in the school band. The guests froze, as if someone had stopped a movie while it was running. Jenny covered Morgan's ears. With a sizzling explosion and a shudder that shook the house, all the lights popped out at once.

8

"Someone wanted to stop our wedding!"

For a long minute, no one said anything. It seemed as if the wind had eaten the last of the daylight outside. Now it was battering the house to let the dark in. Morgan started crying and Jenny's mother shouted, "Paul—where's the baby?"

"He's over here!" Jenny called to her mother. "I've got him."

Then everyone started talking at once. People were bumping into each other. Jenny huddled against the wall and pressed Morgan against her chest, rubbing his back. "It's okay," she said, "don't be scared." But Jenny was shivering all over.

A cigarette lighter flickered under Aunt Grace's round face. Then Jenny's mother lit the candles on the mantel and Charlie Streeter came through the doorway from the kitchen carrying a lantern.

Morgan pointed. "Dat?" he asked, and hiccuped.

"That's a light," Jenny told him, but she was watching Nana. Her grandmother looked frightened. Little shadows flickered across her face as the Gray Man came toward them with the lantern swinging.

"The storm's getting worse," he said. His voice was loud. "Maybe we'd better stay here tonight."

Jenny held her breath, waiting to hear what Nana would say. Her grandmother tossed her head. "Nonsense," she said. "If we can get across the bridge to the mainland, we'll be fine."

Jenny followed the Gray Man and her grandmother into the kitchen. Jenny's fa-

70

ther was standing in the doorway. Water streamed from his yellow slicker.

"The storm's pretty fierce, Lucinda," he called out. "A branch broke off the big spruce tree and tore out the power to the house. Couldn't we persuade you to wait until morning?"

Nana's mouth was set in a hard, firm line. "Afraid not," she said. "It will be an adventure. I'll just run and get my things." She went upstairs, with her sisters following behind her.

Jenny found her mother and pushed Morgan into her arms. "He's wet," she said, and hurried into the laundry room. She fumbled around in the candlelight for her slicker. When she came out, Cody was singing, "Here comes the bride!"

The guests made a path for Nana and the Gray Man. Jenny watched for a minute. The Gray Man was handing their suitcases to Uncle Teto, who set them outside on the screen porch. Nana was crying and hugging everyone. Someone threw a handful of rice; it spattered into Jenny's hair and crunched under her feet when she walked.

"Watch the candles, y'all," Uncle Teddy cried.

Jenny edged toward the door. A flashlight bobbed in the yard and disappeared into the shed. Then the red backup lights of the Gray Man's car came on, and Uncle Teto drove up to the door. Jenny could barely hear the cans and jugs rattle under the howl of the wind.

She went out onto the porch. Nana's duffel was waiting near the door. Jenny picked it up. It swung heavily against her legs.

"Here, let me take that," Teto said, pushing the screen door open. Water dripped from the brim of his baseball cap.

Jenny took a breath. "Nana wants you," she lied. "I can carry it out."

Teto hesitated, then smiled. "You're my helper today, aren't you?" he said. "If it's too heavy, just leave it there."

"Someone wanted to stop our wedding!"

When he disappeared into the kitchen, Jenny stumbled out into the rain. She swallowed hard. First she'd lied to Nana, now to Uncle Teto—

"It's all your fault, you dumb Gray Man," Jenny muttered, struggling with the duffel. The bag knocked into her shins and dragged through a puddle as she hoisted it onto the car. Jenny looked back at the house. Everyone was huddled around Nana and Charlie Streeter. Their bodies looked like thick ghosts wavering in the lantern light.

Jenny climbed into the car, pushed the duffel into the backseat, and then scrambled after it. She curled up on the floor, pulling Nana's wool coat over her. Rain drummed on the roof of the car. There was a roaring pounding in the distance. Jenny tried to imagine what the ocean must look like. She thought about *Georgie Girl,* her father's lobster boat, and wondered if it would be smashed against the pier.

Suddenly she heard shouting, then the

car doors opened and the light came on overhead. Jenny tightened her arms around her knees and held her breath.

"What's going on here, Charlie?" she heard her father yell. "Looks like you're towing beach garbage—and what's this sign on the back—*Not Married?* Someone doesn't approve of the wedding, I guess."

"It looks like Jenny's artwork," Nana said. "Did she do this?"

"With a little help from her friends." That was Teto's deep voice. "Get in the car, Mama," Teto said. "You're getting soaked."

"But where *is* Jenny?" Nana's voice sounded shaky. "You know I can't leave without saying good-bye to her. Where on earth could she be?"

"She must be hiding in the house," her mother said. "Don't worry, Mama. I'll tell her you said good-bye. You can call her later."

"What if the phones go out?" Nana cried.

"Mama, do you have to be so stubborn? Don't leave now." Uncle Teto's voice boomed out over the wind. "New York will wait for you."

"He's right, Mama." Jenny's mother sounded cross too. "Couldn't you stay until the storm is over?"

"It's sure to clear by the time we get to Portland," Nana said. "Now close that door. You'll ruin my dress."

"Don't worry, Bea," Charlie Streeter said. "We'll be back in five minutes if it's not safe."

Jenny listened while everyone said good-bye about ten times. Then the doors slammed. Uncle Teto and Jenny's mother started to sing the family good-bye song but their voices faded as the engine started up.

Jenny's eyes were open but it was dark under the coat. As the car began to roll down the driveway, the cans rattled against the road.

"What's that?" Charlie Streeter ex-

"Someone wanted to stop our wedding!"

claimed, slamming on the brake. Jenny
lurched against the seat. She clutched the
coat tightly over her head as the Gray Man
opened his door, then closed it.

"Those kids," Charlie Streeter said,
starting up again, "they've tied all kinds of
junk to our bumper."

Nana laughed. "Leave it," she said. "No
one will notice in this storm." She coughed
a little. "Charlie, I'm worried about Jenny.
I'm surprised she wouldn't come out to say
good-bye. Do you think she's angry with
me?"

Jenny shifted carefully, straining to hear
over the knocking of the cans.

"No, she's angry with *me*," Charlie
Streeter was saying, "and I don't blame
her. After all, I'm taking you away."

The car moved slowly. In her dark tent,
Jenny waited for Nana to say something,
but all she heard was the crunch of stones,
then the smooth hiss of wet pavement. The
windshield wipers thumped and swished.
She tried to get comfortable, but the hump

on the floor of the car pushed up against her ribs. The Honda trembled as it splashed through puddles.

"Holy Toledo, Lucinda!" Charlie Streeter exclaimed. "Can you believe we got married on a day like this?"

"Maybe you got more than you bargained for," Nana said. They were both talking loudly above the roar of the wind.

"I couldn't ask for anything better, and you know it," Charlie Streeter said.

"But a hurricane!" Nana cried. "If I were superstitious, I might think someone wanted to stop our wedding."

"That's nonsense," the Gray Man said.

Jenny didn't want to hear anymore. She put her fingers in her ears and squinched her eyes tight, trying to keep the tears from oozing out.

9

Stowaway

"Charlie, watch out!"

Nana's sharp cry startled Jenny. Had she fallen asleep? Before she could peek out to see how far they'd gone, tires squealed and the car lurched forward, then plunged down. There was a terrible scraping noise and Jenny was rolled back and forth like a sausage in a pan. The car shuddered, then stopped.

Jenny untangled herself from the coat and sat up slowly, rubbing her bruised knees and elbows. The car was tipped downhill with its back end up in the air.

Jenny peered through the space between the front seats. In the dim light from the dashboard, she could see her grandmother and the Gray Man staring straight ahead out the window. Charlie Streeter's hands gripped the steering wheel and Nana's head was bent down toward her chest. The windshield wipers clacked steadily against the rain.

"They're dead," Jenny whimpered.

But Nana jumped and let out a little scream as if she'd been wakened from a bad dream. Charlie Streeter whirled his head around to stare at Jenny.

"Well, what do you know?" he said. "We've got a stowaway." Jenny cringed, expecting him to get cross, but he just shook his head and gave her a quick, sad smile.

Jenny climbed up onto the backseat. Her arms and legs were prickly from lying scrunched in a ball. She waited for Nana to say something, but her grandmother just sat there, rubbing her wrist with her hand.

"Did we crash?" Jenny asked in a small voice.

No one answered her. Instead, the Gray Man unbuckled his seat belt and leaned over to Nana. "Are you hurt?" he asked.

"I slammed my hand against the dashboard." Nana's voice was shaky, as if she were trying not to cry. "I sprained my wrist, I think—but, Charlie, what will we do now? If only I hadn't been such a stubborn fool! Why did I ever say we should go?"

"Because you're a determined woman who wouldn't let a storm get in her way." Charlie Streeter squeezed Nana's shoulder. "We're in a pretty fix—but never mind. Let's see if we can get out of here." He switched off the engine and turned on the inside light.

"What happened?" Jenny asked, trying to keep her voice from trembling.

"We made it to the north end of the island, but the bridge is flooded," the Gray Man said. "I saw the tide coming right over the top. I braked too fast, and skidded off the road."

"Will the ocean come into my house?"

"Don't worry about your place, hon," Charlie Streeter said. "It's been on that hill for a hundred years. But I'd better take a look at the water here. It might be a little too close for comfort." He wiggled the handle of his door, then shoved against the frame with his shoulder, but it wouldn't open.

"Swains are home, across the road," Nana said suddenly. "I saw a light in their window, just before we crashed. Maybe they can help us."

Jenny was relieved to hear her grandmother speak in a normal voice, but the next minute Nana whirled around in her seat and said angrily, "As for you, young lady—you'd better have a good explanation for what you're doing here."

Jenny huddled against the seat, bracing her feet to keep herself from sliding forward. Didn't Nana love her anymore? She started to cry.

"I didn't mean to!" Jenny cried. "I didn't know it would be so bad."

"Now what on earth does that mean?" Nana exclaimed.

Charlie Streeter put his hand on Nana's knee. "Don't be cross with her now, Lucinda," he said. "We've got more serious things to think about. My door is wedged shut against a boulder."

Nana tried to open her door, but it banged open just a few inches. She stuck her arm outside. "There's a tree here," she said, feeling around in the dark.

The wind was roaring again. Nana and Charlie Streeter were both shouting to hear each other. The Gray Man rolled his window down and tried to climb out, puffing and grunting. Rain came pouring in.

"Charlie, don't be a fool!" Nana cried. "You'll never fit."

Jenny thought about Pooh Bear, who ate so much at Rabbit's house that he got stuck going out the door of the rabbit hole. Charlie Streeter's big bottom waggled next to the steering wheel as he tried to lift himself through the open window. He twisted and groaned, then let himself back down. "Can't do it," he said. "I'm too fat. And I lost my hat out there." His bald spot glistened with rain.

"Let me try," Nana said. She started to climb out her own window, but flopped back quickly, brushing twigs from her hair. "Ouch—my wrist is too sore," she said, "and there are branches up against the window. What will we do?"

"Make a magic trick," Jenny said softly.

Charlie Streeter laughed. "You're the magician today," he said, "sneaking into our car."

"I could get out," Jenny said. When no one answered, she leaned between the front seats and said loudly, "I can fit through the window."

84

"And then what?" Nana said sharply. "I can't let you run around in this storm."

"I don't think we have much choice, Cinda," Charlie said. "Look."

He pointed at the car's headlights. One beamed crazily up into the trees, but the other aimed down into the channel. In the spot where the water usually ran smooth and slick, bringing the tides in and out of Bright's Cove, waves were churning. Foam and spray boiled just below the car.

"The tide's still coming in," Charlie said loudly, checking his watch. "Have you ever seen it so high?"

"In 1938," Nana said, "maybe in '79— you're right, we're going to be trapped." She pulled a flashlight out of the glove compartment and gave it to Jenny. "You'll have to run across the road to Swain's," she said. "Be very careful. Stay away from the trees." She twisted in her seat. Her eyes were big and wet, like a dog's. "Bang on the Swains' door. If no one's home, you come right back, understand? No more foolishness."

Jenny's face felt hot. It was all her fault. They never would have crashed if she hadn't made that wish. Suddenly Jenny wanted to tell her grandmother everything. She couldn't keep swallowing the words down. "Nana—" she blurted, but the Gray Man pulled on her arm.

"I don't want to scare you, hon, but you'd better hurry," he said.

So Jenny zipped her raincoat and sidled through the space between the seats.

"Go out my side," the Gray Man said. "You can climb onto that rock. Here, right over my lap." He rolled his window down. The wind slapped Jenny's face. She ducked her head and pulled her hood up, balancing on Charlie Streeter's legs.

"You're a brave girl," the Gray Man said. "Out you go, now." He held the flashlight while Jenny wriggled out on her belly, feeling for the boulder with her hands. When she was perched on the rock, Charlie

Streeter handed her the flashlight. "Can you see where you're going?" he yelled.

"Sort of." Jenny slid to the ground. The wind came at her like some big bear, tossing her from side to side with its paws. Jenny was frightened. She wanted to cuddle up on Nana's lap with her thumb in her mouth. Instead, she gripped the flashlight and aimed it toward the cove. A wave hissed on the stones just below the front wheels. "I'll be right back," she cried, and scrambled up the bank to the road.

10

"Stop that kissing!"

Jenny hesitated for a minute at the edge of the pavement, trying to listen for cars, but the wind was howling. Wet leaves raced past the beam of her flashlight. Jenny shivered, planting her feet in the wet dirt. Would the wind blow her away, too?

Jenny opened her raincoat and found the silky softness of the rabbit's foot. There was only one wish left. If she used it to rescue her grandmother, Nana would go away with Charlie Streeter. But if she didn't . . .

Jenny hesitated a minute, her legs braced against the wind. The rain beat into her face, and she imagined the little Honda swept into the sea.

"Please," she shouted at last, gripping the rabbit's foot, "don't let Nana drown. Help me save her." Jenny ran and stumbled across the road, her body buffeted by the wind. She only knew she'd found the other side when the hard pavement ended and her sneakers squished and sank in the soggy grass.

She squinted into the darkness. Even though the Swains lived right below Jenny's, the storm made everything look different. Where was their house? Jenny shivered and jabbed her flashlight in different directions. She was about to whirl back toward the road when she saw a yellow globe of watery light in the distance. "Go away, Wanda!" she cried, in case the charm still had magic. But the storm snatched her words away.

She leaned into the wind, trudging toward the light. She found the rabbit's foot again and stroked it for comfort. Suddenly, her feet started acting funny. The ground was moving up and down. Jenny tripped and fell. The wet pine needles under her hands and knees were heaving. First the earth humped up, like Max arching his back after a nap, then it dropped. Was this what an earthquake felt like?

Jenny started to cry. She scrambled to her feet and ran forward. Branches clacked and clattered overhead. Then she saw the wavering light again, gleaming in the front window of the house. Jenny stumbled up the steps and pounded on the door.

When no one answered, she tried the handle. The door flung open and she fell into the house, bumping into old Mr. Swain.

"What on earth—" he exclaimed, grabbing her arm to steady her. His bushy white eyebrows wiggled when he peered under her hood. "Why, Jenny Lawrence—

91

what are you doing here? We thought you'd all be over to your grandma's."

"We were," Jenny said, trying to talk through her sobs. "But Nana and Charlie—they're trapped—the tide's coming up—"

"Steady," Mr. Swain said. He closed the door and called, "Mark—Jenny Lawrence is here needing help!"

There were heavy steps on the stairs as Mark Swain came down, carrying a big flashlight. Soon they were grabbing coats and boots from the hall closet. "Got your breath yet?" Mr. Swain asked Jenny. He pulled an old, crumpled handkerchief from his pocket. "Here you go," he said.

Jenny wiped her face and blew her nose. "Their car went off the road," she said. "They can't get out. And the ocean's almost touching their wheels."

"Anyone hurt?" Mr. Swain asked.

"Nana sprained her wrist," Jenny said. Her teeth were chattering. "And the Honda's wedged against a big rock—"

"We'll take the wrecker," Mr. Swain said.

Jenny smiled through her tears. She'd always wanted to ride in the Swain's big red tow truck. Mr. Swain took Jenny's hand and led her across the yard to the driveway. Mark Swain came behind them, shining his flashlight. As they hurried under the big spruce trees, Jenny felt the ground sway again.

"Glory day!" Mr. Swain yelled. "The spruces want to uproot themselves. Run!"

"Are we having an earthquake?" Jenny shouted.

"Not likely," Mr. Swain explained when they reached the truck. "It's the roots of these trees—they grow so shallow. When the wind tugs their trunks, it makes the roots move right under the ground. Seems like the earth might open up, don't it?"

Jenny nodded. She was relieved when Mark Swain hoisted her into the cab and then climbed into the driver's seat. The

"Stop that kissing!"

engine started with a roar. "Which way?" he said.

"Right over there," Jenny said, pointing. She sat up on her knees behind the gearshift. "Aren't you going to turn on your red lights?" she asked.

"Why, sure." Mark Swain flicked a switch. Red circles swirled in front of them as they edged down the driveway and across the road.

"You came across in this wind all by yourself?" Mr. Swain asked.

Jenny nodded.

"Guess you've got spunk, like your grandma," he said.

Jenny smiled, feeling proud. They crossed the road. When Jenny was alone in the wind, the highway had seemed to go on forever. Now it was just a narrow strip of pavement, cluttered with branches.

"Lucky you didn't get beamed on the head with one of those," Mark Swain said, swerving to avoid a broken limb.

The red brake lights of Charlie Streeter's little car glowed in the rain.

"There it is!" Jenny cried.

While the Swains turned their truck around and backed it slowly toward the Honda, Jenny got out and ran to the car. She pulled back a minute, shocked at what she saw. The inside light was still on. Nana and the Gray Man were locked together like the teenagers who parked near Jenny's house on Saturday nights. Jenny pounded on the window.

"Stop that!" she cried into the wind. "Stop that kissing. You're getting rescued!"

11

A Heart Like
Silly Putty

The Swains lowered the long cable from the winch at the back of the truck and hitched two big metal hooks to the Honda. The Gray Man stuck his head out the window. "Just in time!" he yelled, pointing toward the water. Waves were slapping the front wheel.

"Careful now," Mark Swain called to his father. "If we lose her, she's likely to pitch into the brink."

How did Mark Swain know the Honda was a girl? Jenny wondered. She climbed back into the cab to watch. Mark Swain stood by the Honda, waving his arms and shouting directions while his father worked the winch. The Honda trembled as the cable grew tight. Nana's and Charlie's heads bobbed and jiggled above their seat rests.

The Honda finally moved. It scraped over the rocks, then its hind end rose and the car dangled from the wrecker like a bug. Jenny cheered when the Swains got the Honda out onto the road and lowered it down. Nana and Charlie Streeter stumbled out into the rain, huddling together while the Swains towed the battered car into their driveway and tried to start it. The engine coughed, then stopped.

"Guess she's all wet and tuckered out, like her driver," Mark Swain said, nodding at Charlie Streeter. "You'd better leave her here. Pa, you want to keep watch on the house? I'll drive them home."

At first, Jenny felt warm and excited, sitting on Nana's lap with her legs squeezed against the gearshift. The truck's emergency lights tossed red circles out toward the waving trees and its big engine thrummed. The wind had died a little. "Must be the eye of the storm," Mark Swain said.

"What does that mean?" Jenny asked.

"There's a calm place in the middle of a big storm," Mark Swain explained. "It's quiet for a while—and then she starts up again. Wanda's a right mean lady. A lot of people will be missing their boats, come morning. A big storm like this can break up boats like matchsticks, or draw them out to sea."

Jenny's heart thumped. How could her father catch lobsters if the *Georgie Girl* sank? A sour taste came up in the back of her throat. She slipped her thumb into her mouth, but it didn't comfort her. If only she could take back all her wishes!

They turned the corner into Nana's driveway. A police car sat in front of the house with its blue lights flashing.

"Looks like there's more excitement here," Mark Swain said.

"What on earth—?" Nana exclaimed, but Jenny knew why the police had come.

"They're looking for me," she whimpered, huddling into her coat. She wished she could disappear.

Mark Swain jumped out, leaving the light on inside the cab. When Charlie Streeter opened the truck door, Jenny clutched Nana.

"I won't go out there!" she screamed. She clung to her grandmother, her shoulders heaving. Even with her eyes closed, she could see the storm, an angry monster that had torn out the wires at Nana's house, pushed the Gray Man's car off the road, and made the ocean wild.

"I didn't mean to!" Jenny cried. "I didn't know Wanda would be so big."

Nana leaned over and called out, "Charlie—go tell them we've found her. Close the door—we'll be out in a minute."

Nana eased Jenny gently down onto the

seat beside her. "What are you talking about?" Nana asked.

"The s-storm," Jenny stuttered. "I brought Wanda. I didn't want you to get married," she wailed, and she buried her head on Nana's shoulder.

Nana stroked her hair. "I know you didn't," she said. "But, Jenny, people can't make hurricanes."

"I did," Jenny wailed, her voice muffled against Nana's coat. "I wished on my lucky charm—the rabbit's foot I found at O'Leary's."

"Jen." Nana propped Jenny up so she could look into her face. Her eyes were dark and serious. "What you did was wrong, coming in our car without telling anybody. You've made everyone worry terribly. But you can't control a storm. Believe me. Even a powerful little girl like you can't tell a hurricane what to do."

"Yes I did," Jenny insisted. The words came rushing out in a torrent, like the rain drumming on the roof of the cab. "The

101

rabbit's foot works," she sobbed. "Look." She unhooked the charm from her pants and held it in the palm of her hand. The fur was wet and grimy. Jenny stared at it a second, then dropped it on the seat, as if it had suddenly come alive.

"First I wished for the hurricane," Jenny explained, "and it came. Then I wished that you wouldn't leave Bright's Island"— she gulped—"and you crashed. Charlie Streeter said there were always three wishes—" Jenny could hardly speak, she was crying so hard, but she forced the words out. "I had one wish left, so I asked the rabbit's foot to help me rescue you."

"Oh, Jen," Nana said, "the storm and the accident were both just bad luck. And the rabbit's foot didn't save us. *You* did. You're the one who crossed the road in the wind. You're brave, Jen, that's all there is to it."

Jenny buried her head on her grand-mother's chest and they sat still for a long time. She cried and cried while Nana stroked her hair.

"Dear heart," Nana said at last, "I'm afraid you can't stop me from going away. We'll stay tonight, but we'll have to leave as soon as the storm is over. Charlie's taking me to San Francisco. He told me while we were waiting in the car."

"I know," Jenny wailed, sobbing again. "I threw your brochures into the ocean—" Her breath was tangled up in her chest and she couldn't say anything else.

Nana laughed. "I don't need them—I'll see the city with my own eyes in a few days."

Jenny scrubbed her eyes with her fists. The wishes were all used up, and Nana was married. There was nothing else she could do. She clutched her hands against her chest, trying to stop the cold, sharp needles jabbing at her heart. "I don't want you to live so far away."

"I know you don't," Nana said quietly. "And it makes me sad, too."

A Heart Like Silly Putty

Jenny looked up at her grandmother. "It does?"

Nana nodded. Her eyes were bright with tears and her mouth trembled a little. "It's a big change for me. I'm going to miss you terribly—you and Morgan and your mom and dad. I've lived at the far end of the island ever since you were born."

Jenny cuddled up to her grandmother. Somehow, knowing Nana would miss her eased the ache that had spread all through her bones.

"I didn't realize how lonesome I was until Charlie started coming around. He made me laugh and look forward to things," Nana said.

Jenny sighed. How could Nana be lonely when she and Morgan came to see her almost every day? Sometimes she just didn't understand grown-ups.

"You'll like New York better than Maine," Jenny said sadly. "Uncle Teto lives there."

Nana laughed. "Not a chance," she said.

"New York's exciting, but I'll bet no one in the whole city knows about mischief days. With Charlie and Teto in New York and you Lawrences in Maine, my heart will be in two places at once. Hearts can expand, you know." She put her hand on her chest. "Why, mine feels so big now, I'll bet it can stretch from Bright's Island all the way to New York."

"Like Silly Putty," Jenny said. "No matter how far you pull it, it won't break."

"Exactly," Nana said, and she laughed. "Better give me that rabbit's foot. It's caused enough trouble. When we go through Stone Harbor tomorrow, I'll toss it out the window. Send it back where it belongs."

"That's littering," Jenny scolded, wiping her tears.

"Well, if it is, that's just too bad." Nana put the rabbit's foot in her coat pocket. "Now listen. You get out and tell your mother and father you're sorry. I'll explain everything. And then, we'll see if we can't get the party going again." She tossed her head. Her cheeks were bright red, as if she'd been out in the cold too long.

"I have to tell you, I'm a little embarrassed myself," Nana admitted. "Causing a wreck, and bringing the Swains out on a night like this." She gave Jenny a quick hug. "Come on, girl. It's like that old song. We'll face the music, and then we'll dance."

12

The Wind That Danced the Samba

The door opened and Jenny tumbled out into her father's arms. "Where did you go?" he demanded, his voice croaking like an old bullfrog. "We've been looking everywhere for you."

Jenny was afraid. Her father's eyes were wild looking and his thin blond hair was plastered to his forehead. He squeezed her hard against his chest before setting her down. Jenny's mother appeared from the darkness, grabbed Jenny by the shoulders and shook her, crying, "Don't you ever,

ever do that again!" Jenny's teeth chattered. She tried to say she was sorry, but she was crying too hard.

"Hold on, Bea," the Gray Man said. He put his arm around Jenny's mother. "I know how you've worried. But your little girl saved our lives."

In spite of herself, Jenny gave the Gray Man a quick smile. It was nice of him to stand up for her.

"I don't understand." Jenny's mother stared at Charlie Streeter, then at Nana, her face pinched tight. "What on earth happened?"

Before anyone could explain, they heard the sound of boots squelching in the wet grass. Jenny found herself surrounded by Nana's relatives and friends. They stared at her and then peppered her with questions. The policeman came up behind Peter and Cody. He swept the yellow beam of his flashlight across Jenny's face, making her blink.

"She's right here, and she's safe," Jenny's mother said, and Jenny's father apologized for making him come over.

"No trouble at all," the policeman said. "I'm just glad no one was hurt."

"No trouble at all," Peter mimicked, sneering at Jenny. "Bet you thought it was fun, making us think you'd drowned."

Jenny stuck out her tongue at him.

"Now wait a minute," Nana said. "If it weren't for Jenny, Charlie and I would be lobster bait. Go on, Jen, explain what happened."

Standing in the rain, Jenny told the story from the beginning: how she'd hidden in the Gray Man's car, how she'd climbed out the window and crossed the road to the Swains. When she described the way the ground moved up and down under the spruce trees even Peter seemed impressed. Jenny's father patted her on the head and her mother was laughing and crying at the same time, squeezing Jenny's hand as if she might never let go.

"You skunk!" Uncle Teto cried. "I

guessed you'd stowed away in that car—but no one believed me."

Cody put his hand on Jenny's shoulder. "You are braver than I thought," he said.

"It was scary in the wind," Jenny admitted, and as she spoke a gust hit them so hard that they all knocked into each other like pins at the bowling alley.

"Wanda's back!" Nana screamed.

"Last one in lights the candles," Teto yelled, and they ran for the house.

Back inside, Aunt Grace fussed over Nana's swollen wrist while everyone peeled off wet coats and hats. Aunt Sarah gave Nana a heavy sweater to pull on over her dress.

"I believe I could eat something!" Charlie Streeter exclaimed. Uncle Teddy poured him a mug of hot coffee and took him into the dining room to make a sandwich. Jenny's mother brought more candles from the kitchen. The room was crowded; Mark Swain was shaking hands with Aunt Sarah and all the relatives clustered at the table for a snack. Nana came in holding an ice pack on her wrist.

"Lucinda, look behind you," Charlie Streeter said. Nana turned around: Uncle Teto stood in the doorway carrying the wedding cake.

"We were in such a hurry to send you off, we forgot your cake," Uncle Teto said, setting it on the table. Nana and Charlie Streeter admired the creamy white layers topped with a tiny ballerina and a young bridegroom in a black coat.

"That poor groom doesn't get enough to eat," Charlie Streeter said, touching the plastic figure. "Better cut this cake, and we'll fatten him up."

Everyone clapped when Nana and the Gray Man took the long knife and sliced through the cake from top to bottom. Uncle Teddy poured champagne and sparkling cider while Jenny and her mother passed the plates. Nana held up her glass and tapped the rim. Golden bubbles sifted down through the glittering liquid.

The Wind That Danced the Samba

"I propose a toast to Wanda!" Nana cried. "With thanks for giving us a little more time at the party." The wind howled and Nana laughed. "She's talking to us. No one's going home tonight."

"I'm not sleeping upstairs," Aunt Grace cried, as the shutters rattled against the side of the house. "What if the roof caves in?"

"We'll have a slumber party right here in the dining room," Uncle Teddy boomed. "Anyway, I don't think Lucinda and Charlie want you upstairs with them."

Jenny stared at the Gray Man. "Are you going to sleep in Nana's room?" she blurted.

The Gray Man's face turned bright red and the cousins whistled. "I was planning on it," he said.

"You won't fit in her bed, will you?" Jenny asked.

"Jenny!" Nana warned. "Enough is enough. Remember what I said?"

Jenny turned away and wound her arms

113

tight around her stomach, trying to keep the laughter from bursting out. Uncle Teto winked at her. His mouth was hidden in his beard but she could tell he was covering up a laugh too. Jenny grinned. Later on, when no one was listening, she would tell Uncle Teto about the Gray Man getting stuck in the window of his Honda.

"Mattresses all over the floor, people sleeping at the foot of the bed," Uncle Teddy said. He was pulling his banjo case out from underneath the table. "Doesn't that put a song in y'all's head?"

The cousins went for their instruments. The wind was whining like a dog shut out in the cold. The candles sputtered and Mark Swain cried, "Here she comes!"

Jenny laughed. Hondas and hurricanes were both girls to Mark Swain.

Uncle Teddy tuned his banjo. Guitar cases snapped open as he twisted the pegs, inching the notes a little higher. Uncle Teddy played slowly at first, then sped up until his fingers were a blur over the strings.

"Whoo-ee!" Mark Swain called out. He tapped his foot while they sang about kinfolks coming to visit and filling up the house. *"You knowed darn well when night comes on, you was headed for the foot of the bed,"* the man in the song complained.

"They tell me some folks don't know how it is, having company all over the place; to rassle for a cover through a long winter night, with a big foot settin' in your face," Jenny sang, rocking back and forth on the soles of her feet. *"Cold toenails a-scratchin' your back, and a footboard scrubbin' your head . . ."*

Cody and Peter were strumming fast, watching Uncle Teddy to keep the beat. Aunt Sarah played the ukelele. Her painted fingernails tweaked the strings. Jenny stole a look at Nana. Aunt Grace was wrapping her grandmother's wrist in a long, stretchy bandage, but Nana didn't

even notice. She was holding Charlie
Streeter's hand and looking up into his
face. Jenny watched them, feeling happy
and sad all at once.

Suddenly, she ran to Nana and put her
arms around her grandmother's waist. The
Gray Man squeezed Jenny's shoulder.
"Quite an adventure we had together," he
said.

Instead of pulling away, Jenny grinned
up at him. "Almost as good as a mischief
day," she said.

The Gray Man laughed, and leaned over
her head to kiss Nana so that Jenny was
sandwiched between them. She wriggled
free as the music stopped.

"Bravo!" Nana cried. "Play another
song. It's time to dance!"

"Lucinda," Aunt Grace scolded, "your
wrist is badly sprained already!"

But Nana stepped lightly from a chair
onto the wide butcher-block table, kicking
off her shoes. Uncle Teto caught them,
and clapped the soles together like casta-

nets. Charlie Streeter swayed beside her, whistling.

"Get up there with her!" Uncle Teddy bellowed, slapping Charlie Streeter on the back.

"Not on your life," the Gray Man announced. "Lucinda's the featherweight in this marriage." He tapped his feet to the rhythm of the music and beamed at Nana. His glasses twinkled in the light.

"Come on, Jenny, I need a partner!" Nana cried. Before Jenny knew what was happening, she had pulled off her shoes and climbed up on the table. Nana took Jenny's elbow with her bandaged arm.

"Show off," Peter muttered, but Jenny didn't care. She felt tall and wild, looking down on all the heads.

"Lucinda, you're making a fool of yourself up there," Aunt Grace said as she rushed to move the food out of the way.

"I'm used to being a fool," Nana laughed. "Paul—where are you? Play us a samba!"

Jenny's father brushed his rumpled hair

from his forehead and sat at the old upright piano. He started a tune that rolled and bounced. Peter picked up two spoons from the table and slapped them up and down against his knee. Aunt Sarah disappeared and came back with maracas, two red wooden shakers with seeds inside. They made a soft, sliding beat.

"One two three four Sam-BA!" Jenny's father sang, his fingers trilling over the keyboard.

Jenny bounced with the music, her feet moving as fast as Cody's hand, which rolled over the guitar strings in a blur.

Everyone started to dance. Heads bobbed and swayed around the table. Even Aunt Grace waggled her hips from side to side when Cody sang, "Can you dance the SamBA?" Jenny's mother sidled across the room, swinging Morgan in her arms. He squealed, his blue eyes wide.

Jenny and Nana whirled on their tiny dance floor as the music went faster and faster.

"Yes, I dance the Sam-BA!" Jenny sang, stomping her foot every time her father hit the loud, final beat. The music thawed the last cold place around her heart.

Jenny looked up at Nana. Her grandmother's face was flushed and her eyes were dancing as fast as her feet. "Sometimes we're sad," Nana cried out, "but then sometimes, we dance!"

Jenny jumped into the air, clicking her heels. And then she heard other music, louder than the roll of her own feet on the table, louder than the rollicking harmonies of all the instruments hurrying over the chords. Outside the house, following its own syncopated beat, Wanda the hurricane was dancing the samba too, keeping time with the rain and the waves as they pounded the shore of the cove.